A LITTLE *winter* FLING

LISAMARIE KADE

one

. . .

"Come on, Marina!" my best friend all but shouts.

"Fine, fine. Call me a stalker, but I am going to stare until that fine-ass specimen is out of sight."

I do not care what she says; that man is fine. Dark hair that looks to be styled just right. He's too far away to tell what color eyes he has, but if I had to guess, I would go with an almond or chocolate color.

We walk into Gravity Ski Hill, the Breckenridge ski lodge, and find a warm place to sit down while waiting for a notification that our room is ready.

I spot the dark and oh-so-handsome dude the second we walk through the large doors. He is hard to miss. "That's better," I quip as we sit down in one of the many oversized chairs.= placed throughout the lobby. Callia and I could share one, that is how big they are.

I do not want to make it obvious that I am checking him out. I try to focus on the artwork, but that is boring stuff. I glance back in his direction, and to my surprise, he is looking at me. Holy shit! He just smiled. I feel my cheeks heat as I quickly turn to look at Callia.

"Oh my God, Callia. He looked at me. Like looked at me and smiled."

My best friend looks up from her cell phone and shakes her head while rolling her eyes.

"You are crazy."

I shrug my shoulders. "Maybe, but you put up with me."

"This is true."

I smile before turning in his direction once more. Yes, I am crazy.

"Room is ready, let's go," Callia says as she stands. She wastes no time sauntering in the man's direction.

He stands and begins walking toward us. Is he coming this way on purpose? As he gets closer, I notice his pants are fitted just right in the thighs. He's muscular, no doubt.

"Hello, ladies," he purrs, his accent strong. He must be from somewhere in the United Kingdom.

I stop dead in my tracks while Callia keeps on going. Her steps never falter. She's no fun.

"Well, hello there," I reply confidently.

"Excuse me for being so blunt, but I could not help but notice you from across the room."

I know, dude. Me too, me too.

Blush creeps into my cheeks once again as I take

in his appearance. I was close on the eye color. They are dark, black almost.

"What brings you here?" he asks, and I swear my panties start to melt. His damn voice is intoxicating.

"Girls' trip. You?"

"I am on holiday. Just got in."

I nod, unsure of how to respond. Usually, I am quick with talking to a guy, however, there is something about this man.

The man smiles. "I'm Leon, and you are?"

The way the letter L rolls off his tongue. It should be a crime.

"Marina."

I dart my hand out to shake his. His strong hand grips mine and pulls it up to his lips. "May I?"

I nod because quite frankly, it is the only thing I know how to do at the moment. I never thought a man could render me speechless, yet here we are. He kisses the back of my hand lightly. It should not be a big deal. It is no big deal.

Lies, I tell myself.

Leon does not let go of my hand. Instead, he leads me over to those big chairs and we sit together in one.

With our bodies practically touching, I have to remind myself to calm down.

It is just a man, Marina.

Except he is not just any man. He is one with dark hair and eyes that match. A sexy accent and strong hands.

He is way more of a man than any goon back home.

Yes, I'll admit it. I'm over here swooning at Leon.

"Have you been here before?" he asks.

"No." I shake my head while still smiling. "This is my first time here at the lodge. Actually, it is my first time in Colorado."

"I see. I come here every December."

"Really? That is kind of cool, but why?"

"I like an escape before the craziness of the holiday season."

"That is a brilliant idea." I nod.

It is a genius idea. The only reason we came out here before Christmas was because the flight was cheap, and I needed to get away before having to deal with my family. My family thinks I should be married and knocked up already. They do not understand that I am twenty-five and that is not the life I want.

"How long are you here for?" Leon asks, snapping me back to reality.

"Six days."

"So, I have six days to get to know you." The tone of his voice tells me he is making a statement. There's a sparkle in his eyes.

"Yup, that is all you get," I flirt back. I have no desire for anything more than just a fling. Gosh, any relationship that lasts longer than a month, my parents start questioning marriage.

Someone clears their throat and we both turn to

see Callia standing in front of us. When the heck did she appear?

"Oh, hey, Callia." I smile. "This is Leon. Leon, this is my best friend, Callia."

To my surprise, Leon stands, and instead of shaking Callia's hand, he pulls her in for a hug and a slight kiss on the cheek. What the hell? He didn't kiss my cheek.

"It is a pleasure to meet you," he says.

"Leon is here on holiday," I supply.

My best friend looks from him to me with mischief in her eyes. I know that look. It is the one that says *You are a hussy.* It wouldn't be the first time she's called me that either.

"Our room is ready."

"It's about time!" I clap my hands while jumping to my feet.

But what about Leon?

"Oh, um, Leon. Maybe we can grab a drink or something later?"

I blurt the words out so fast that I don't have time to ask Callia if that would be all right. Leon looks between the two of us.

"What about your plans with your friend?"

I wave my hand. "Callia will be fine. We don't have any plans tonight. Right, Callia?" I look at her and give her my best *I owe you* face.

"She's right. We don't have anything going on this evening. You two should get drinks down in the lounge later."

And that right there is why Callia Martinez is my very best friend.

"Perfect. Say six o'clock? I'll be at the bar, waiting."

"I'll be there." I barely get the words out as he lifts my hand, kissing it once more before walking away.

"Marina!" Callia loudly whispers as we head in the direction of our room.

"I know! I know. I owe you."

She shakes her head at me while smiling. She knows exactly how I am.

When we step onto the elevator, all I can think about is Leon's accent, his eyes. How romantic he seems.

He is swoon-worthy!

And if I'm lucky, I'll get laid tonight.

two

· · ·

I stare at my reflection in the mirror. My dark hair is pulled into a low bun. Not sure I like it, though. I decide to undo the top button of my pink and purple flannel. I think it gives a little flirty vibe. My black jeans hug my hips and ass perfectly. I have been blessed with curves, all thanks to my mama.

Glancing at myself again, still unsatisfied with my hair, I pull out the hair tie and start running my fingers through it.

That is better.

"How do I look?"

"You look fine. Besides, it's not like you are wearing some sexy outfit. We are in Breckenridge, and it's cold."

"So, I still need to look good for Leon."

I dab a little bit of lippy on my lips. I don't know why, but I love to look good next to a man and with Leon looking the way he does, I definitely need to look good on his arm.

Capping my lippy, I walk up to Callia. "Are you sure you are okay with me going out for a little bit?"

"Of course. It is not like we have any plans tonight."

"Yeah, okay. I'm hoping to get some you know, a little winter fling."

Callia laughs. I shrug with a smile plastered across my face. There is no shame in my game.

"Go on now, don't keep the man waiting." She points to the door.

Well, when she says it like that.

"Do you want me to bring you back anything? Should I be back for dinner?"

"No, I'll eventually head down and see what there is. Worse case, I can order something to be delivered."

I nod. "All right, girl. If you change your mind, shoot me a text."

As soon as the door clicks shut, I pick up my pace. I am itching for a little fun. I know it was not in my plans. I had sworn we were leaving all our problems behind when we got here. Really, we have left them behind, and I promise myself that I won't create any new problems. Leon is just a fling. Nothing more. Besides, after I leave here, I'll most likely never see him again.

I have sworn off relationships and anything that comes with the word love. While my parents are partially to blame for that, they are not entirely at fault.

Too many failed relationships. Too many lies. No one can hurt me if I do not commit.

I see Leon as soon as I step out of the elevator. He is hard to miss. Tall, dark, and oh so delicious. I hope he is as good in bed as he looks.

I wave as I approach him. Something flashes in his eyes. He is probably hoping he will get laid tonight. And he will.

He just doesn't know it yet.

"Marina," he says before pulling me into an embrace.

Wow! He smells so good. He must be wearing Dior, or maybe it's Dolce & Gabbana. Does not matter. His cologne alone is enough to turn a girl on.

"Hey," I reply as casually as I possibly can.

I am still distracted by whatever cologne he is wearing when he pulls away to link his arm around my back, his hand only an inch or so away from my ass.

Yes, it turns me on. Like I said, no shame.

"Is your friend okay on her own?"

"Callia, yeah. She's good."

"I do hope I am not disrupting your plans."

"Not at all."

Leon nods his head as we enter the lounge. He walks us to a corner spot at the bar and holds out the high-back stool. I smile and take a seat, hoping I did it gracefully. It is hard being short sometimes.

He passes me a drink menu, and we each look it over in silence. I am currently torn between a mango margarita and a glass of Moscato. The margarita will liven things up. Wine, well, that will put me in a relaxed mood and that is not what I am going for tonight.

Mango margarita it is.

From here, the snow-capped mountains stand tall in the distance as the snow continues to fall. I can hear fire crackling from somewhere and turn to find it. There, on the opposite side of the room, is a very modern looking fireplace. Encased in glass, the flames dance around the logs, their light giving off a golden glow.

The bartender comes to take our drink order. I find myself surprised that Leon ordered a scotch neat. Like, who does that?

So, I ask. "Inquiring minds want to know, why did you order your scotch neat?"

Leon chuckles before giving me a devilish grin. "I like to feel the burn. It reminds me that I am alive."

"You know a woman can make you feel alive too." I run my hand down his arm.

Well, hot damn. I have no idea where that came from. My drink hasn't even been made yet.

The gorgeous man next to me lets out a low and deep chuckle. I like the way it sounds. He says nothing in return, though, and I begin to worry that maybe I have come on too strong.

It happens occasionally. Do I care? Nope.

The bartender returns promptly with our drinks

and leaves us to what feels like our own personal bubble.

I take a sip of my drink. It's good. I look at Leon as he brings the glass to his lips. The amber liquid gently flows into his mouth. How does he make that look sexy? Like seriously, it should be a crime.

When he pulls the glass from his lips, he winks. "Do you think you can make me feel alive?"

Heat floods my face while I squeeze my thighs together. I do not know why his words turn me, yet they do. I shift in my seat, hoping to give him a better view of the hint of cleavage I have going on.

"I can make your wildest fantasies come to life." I return the wink.

"I bet you can," he says, his accent thick.

I smile as I take another sip of my margarita, thinking about the anticipation and the possibilities of later. I picture us naked and a whole lot of sex.

Our time here in the bar needs to hurry up.

three

· · ·

Two drinks in, and I am feeling pretty good. Leon has told me all about where he is from. I was right. He is from the United Kingdom. He lives just outside of Leeds. He told me exactly where, I just did not pay attention because, in my mind, that is not important.

"So, Marina, may I ask your age?"

"I am twenty-five."

Leon nods and swallows thickly. He immediately reaches for his glass of amber liquid and downs it. When he sets his glass down, he gives me a look that I can't quite decipher.

Hmm… I have a feeling things are about to get interesting.

"What? How old are you?"

"I am thirty-nine. About to be forty."

Ooh! An older man. Nothing wrong with that. I like it. I think I like it a lot. If all goes well, I'll know soon enough.

I nod as I take a sip of my drink. "That's cool."

The man next to me looks bewildered.

"What?"

"Does my age not bother you?"

"Not at all, I am a don't knock it until you try it type of girl. As long as my age does not bother you, I don't see an issue."

"I like the way you think, Marina."

A look of what can only be described as relief washes across his features. Thank goodness, because my pride would have taken a hit.

"How is a girl like you not taken?"

Ugh. I hate this part. I get asked it whenever I go out with someone new. It gets old, especially when we both know it is just a hook up, no strings attached. Like, why ask?

"I am happily single," I reply confidently.

Leon nods and rubs his chin. He is pondering his next question. Little does he know, I am ready for it.

"Go on, ask away." I smirk while waving down the bartender.

"I take it someone must have hurt you?"

"Ha!" I scoff. He's not wrong about the hurt part. However, it has been over two years since I let that shit happen. "Once upon a time, maybe." I pause to take a sip of my drink. "I don't want the pressure that comes with dating."

The only thing I need in my life is the occasional one-night stand. My collection of vibrators takes care of the rest.

"Maybe I can change your mind."

He didn't just say what I think he did! I nearly spit my drink back into the glass. What did he just say?!

"Come again?"

Leon sits up a little taller, adjusting himself. "I said, maybe I can change your mind."

I shake my head as laughter escapes my lips. I seriously do not mean to laugh right in his face, but I can't help it.

"That is doubtful," I say matter-of=factly.

"Why is that?"

"Well, for starters, Leon, neither of us reside here. You live across the globe. I live in Florida. There is no chance that you can change my mind."

He laughs. "I think we could work something out."

I shake my head once more. "The only thing to work out is when you plan on taking me back to your room."

Desire fills Leon's dark eyes. He leans in close. His scotch-laced lips are inches from mine. "I have six days to change your mind. Then we will see."

"No way."

"Come on, give me six days." He leans in closer, his lips just grazing mine before he pulls back. It ignites a fire inside of me. My skin prickles. I want more. I want to know what his lips feel like against mine. I want to know what he tastes like when he kisses me.

"You're crazy."

"Quite possibly I am. Time will tell."

And then he pulls back, putting out the inferno that he just lit. Damn him. He leaves me squeezing my thighs harder than I have all night. I can feel my arousal. I am fucking soaked, and the man has not laid a hand on my body yet. When he does, I already know that it will be more than I have ever experienced. I may be in over my head with this man. If he can get me so riled up that I am soaked and already craving his touch when he has never touched me before, yeah, I could very well be in trouble.

We sit there in a comfortable silence, just enjoying our drinks and each other's presence. I will admit, I like it. I feel zero pressure to keep up a conversation.

Shit, maybe it is the tequila that is running through my bones, but I like that we can just be next to each other without the need for words.

I have no idea how much time passes before Leon clears his throat to speak.

"Would you like another drink?"

I shake my head. "I think I am good."

He waves to the bartender who comes our way almost instantly. I go to open my wristlet, but Leon puts a hand over mine. I look up to meet his eyes.

"Let me give you some money."

"No, Marina. Put your money away."

"What? No, I ordered quite a few drinks."

Leon looks at me, his stare nearly penetrating every ounce of my soul. I can't help but hope that he looks at me the same way once he has me naked on his bed.

"I have got it. Now put your money away."

Yes, sir.

Fuck, if I wasn't turned on before, I sure as hell am now. Leon is hot. His accent is hotter. Him making demands to me is the hottest thing ever.

Leon stands from his spot and holds out a hand for me to take. I place my hand in his, excited more than ever to be moving on to our next adventure. An adventure that takes place behind closed doors.

four

. . .

Leon helps me down from my stool and guides me out of the lounge ever so smoothly. His tall frame towers over my short statue. His hand rests on my back once again. It is intimate, and while it makes me feel some sort of way, I do my best to shake it off.

Leon and I are not an item. We are a one-night stand about to happen. Nothing personal. While we walk, I begin to wonder how he is in bed. Is he vanilla? Does he like it rough? All the thoughts swirl with the tequila. It makes me tingle with excitement.

I hope however he is, it will bring me pleasure.

He ushers us down the hall, bypassing the elevator and the large winding marble staircase. This resort is stunning. From the architect down to the interior design, it is just beautiful.

"Where are we going?" I ask.

"To my room. I have a suite on the first floor."

Leon looks down at me and smiles. It is genuine. I do like that about him. Everything about the man seems genuine.

We stop at a door, and he pulls out his room card. Holding the door open, he gestures for me to go in first.

His manners are too good.

Of course, I have established this, yet I keep waiting for him to drop the act of being a gentleman.

"Make yourself comfortable." He walks over to a set of sliding doors and steps out on the patio.

I plan to get comfortable, all right. I waste no time undressing. To be nude is to be comfortable.

After sliding the sheets back, I climb onto the middle of Leon's hotel bed and pull the sheets over me. I sure hope he doesn't mind.

I'm a straight and to-the-point kind of chick.

A slight chill has settled in the room from Leon leaving the patio doors open. I don't mind it, though.

When he comes back in, he takes one look at me. I smile as shock registers. It doesn't last as it is quickly replaced with desire.

"What's this?" he asks, his accent thick. There is a crooked smile on his lips.

"Let's call it dessert. Come to bed and have a taste." I lean up just enough to let the sheets fall past my chest, putting my perky tits on display.

Leon sucks in a breath while admiring me. My nipples pebble at the thought of his mouth on them.

He nods slowly before he begins undressing. It's torture watching him. He removes each piece of clothing at a snail's pace. I could do it for him much faster, but it would probably involve me ripping something, so it is best that I don't.

As soon as he pulls his boxer briefs down his thighs, his erection springs free. Even from here, I can tell he is thick. My mouth salivates, and I can feel my pussy grow wet. I need to feel him now.

"Do you have a condom?" I ask. If he doesn't, I do.

"Yes. "

His back muscles flex as he leans to grab his wallet from the pants he had on. The man has a nice ass too. He is packing the goods in every area. I hope he fucks as good as he looks.

Leon walks up to me, his cock bouncing with each step. I watch as he sets the condom on the nightstand and then crawls over to hover above me. He is so much bigger than me.

"What was that you said about dessert?" His voice is thick with lust. It riles me up.

"I am the dessert." I wink before I lean as far back as the pillows will allow, daring him to take a nipple in his mouth.

In one fluid motion, he wraps a strong arm around my back and leans down. His tongue darts out, circling my nipple. He flicks and swirls, teasing. He switches and repeats the same on my other nipple. My back arches further.

"Leon," I pant. "I want more."

He sits back, and the cool air hits my now wet nipples. It's not cold, though. No, instead, I feel like I am on fire. Hot from the things his mouth was just doing.

"Is that so?"

I nod and go to reach out for his cock. He grabs my wrist, stopping me. I arch an eyebrow in question.

"I'm not done tasting my dessert."

Before I can process the words that just left his mouth, he yanks down the sheets, exposing all of me to him.

Leon licks his lips like a man starved. I know without a doubt that I am about to be eaten like dessert.

five

. . .

My back arches as soon as Leon's lips touch the most sensitive part of my body. His tongue darts between my slit, tasting me.

A moan escapes me as pleasure begins to build. I can't help but squirm under his touch. Leon notices, gripping my hips tighter. He holds me in place while he continues to feast on my delicate flesh. The way his tongue darts out against my clit repeatedly has my toes curling. I know I won't be able to stand it much longer.

His circular motions cause me to squeeze my eyes shut as he brings me to the brink. Out of nowhere, he begins sucking. The sensation is too much. Pleasure rips throughout my entire body. It's as if the stars collide with the ocean, plunging into the darkness that is my orgasm.

Leon continues to lap up every ounce of me while my legs try to squeeze him. I can't help it, though, I have zero control of my body in this state.

My breathing is erratic as the waves of pleasure fade out. I have never come apart like this before. And certainly not by a man's tongue alone. Usually, there's a finger or two to assist. Maybe an older man is the secret I've been missing out on.

That man's hands never left my hips. Even still, right now, his hands are glued to my hips while he peers up at me from between my legs.

"Dessert was delicious."

My mouth drops open. I'm at a loss for words.

I think I have met my match.

Savage. The man is a savage.

"Is that so?" I question. So lame, but it's all I can come up with.

The man nods while climbing over my body. He reaches for the condom, bringing it to his mouth to tear open a corner.

I don't know why I find him using his teeth hot, I just do. I wonder if he fucks as good as he gives giving oral sex.

One thing I am certain of, he is an expert at eating pussy.

Leon settles himself between my legs, and my excitement grows all over again. Just as his tip brushes against my lips, he pauses.

"You want this?"

Is he seriously asking me? He just gave me the best orgasm of my life with his tongue and he wants to know if I want the rest of him. Of course, I want his cock!

"Yes, now fuck me."

As soon as the words leave my mouth, Leon thrusts all the way in, hard. The man doesn't give me time to stretch to take all of him. His hips work in swift movements, pounding into me. The pain mixes with pleasure I have never known. He hits that magical spot with each thrust.

My long purple nails rake down his back as he brings me to the brink of what I know will be another mind-blowing orgasm.

Leon pulls back. His strong hands lift my hips, causing me to throw my legs over his shoulders. A hiss leaves his lips as he thrusts even deeper.

In this position, his cock not only fills me but also hits my g-spot in the most delicious way.

The man must notice when my legs begin to tremble because he quickens his pace.

"Leon!" I scream out as soon as waves of thunderous pleasure rip through me. Moans continue to leave my mouth until Leon's lips seal over mine. He kisses me with a vengeance as he explodes, hammering me hard. His frenzied thrusts slow after a few seconds, leaving behind a dull ache. I know, without a doubt, I will be sore, maybe even bruised tomorrow.

This had to be the most erotic sex of my life.

Never has a man made me come part at his touch in such a way that it leaves me craving more.

"I'm going to run us a shower," he says while climbing off of me.

My phone starts ringing as soon as the words

leave his mouth. I sit up and look in the direction of my purse that holds my phone.

Throwing the sheets back, I climb out of bed, still unashamed to be naked in front of him. My skin is glistening with sweat, a mixture of both of ours, I'm sure.

Yanking my phone out, I see Callia's name on the screen.

"Hey, babe! What's up?" I say as casually as I possibly can.

"Hey, I was just checking in. Everything good on your end?"

"Oh yeah!"

"That's good. Hey, listen, I am going out for a bit." I hear the nervousness in her voice. Little alarm bells start to go off in the back of my head.

"Wait! With who, because I know you aren't going anywhere alone."

"I, uh, met someone while in the market."

"What do you mean? A guy?"

"His name is Dane. We thought it would be fun to go on a fake date." Callia is trying to play it cool. I can hear it in her tone, except I know her a little too well. My friend doesn't do wild things. She leaves the wild for me.

"Callia, are you feeling okay? This is so out of character of you."

"I know."

At least she knows this isn't like her. But me being how I am, I need details. I want to know more.

"Tell me all the things!"

"Marina, chill. It is fine. I am fine. I will tell you everything later."

She ends the call, leaving me hanging. I'm both worried, yet excited for her. Maybe she'll get lucky and find someone to fuck her senseless. Goodness knows she could use a good fuck. Which reminds me.

I walk into Leon's bathroom. Having a suite sure does have some perks. The shower alone is larger than the bathroom in my room.

"I have the shower ready." He nods with a sly smile.

"A shower sounds wonderful."

He takes me by the hand. Excitement grows with each step. It's been ages since I have had shower sex.

And while I have no idea if that is Leon's expectation, it is mine, and I'll make sure it happens.

I already have a plan in place. A plan that involves dropping to my knees.

six

. . .

Steam fills the space between us. Hot water prickles at my skin, yet I welcome it. The man in front of me starts washing my body right away, not giving me a chance to make my move. He runs the soapy white cloth along my skin. I hate to admit that it is soothing.

When Leon reaches between my legs, he is gentle. He must sense how sore I am. It's a good sore, though. And yet not quite sore enough because I want to do it all over again. I reach out for him and run my hands down his chiseled chest. My nails drag downward slightly, pausing when I reach below his stomach. I take my time and admire him. That perfect shape that leads to his cock is delicious. His muscles prominent. Impressive for a man who is nearing his forties. I trace his muscles, watching as he becomes aroused. When I finally grab his cock, taking it in my hands, he hisses.

"Marina." The way my name rolls off his tongue

makes me feel things. I love his accent and the way he says my name.

My eyes flick to his. The lust is there. There is no way to deny it.

"Leon," I say, giving him a wink, and then I drop to my knees.

With the water pouring over our bodies, I stroke him slowly. He is thick and veiny. The thought of me giving him head excites me.

Ever so slowly, I drag my tongue along his shaft. Leon's body sways slightly, causing his hand to dart out against the wall to steady himself. I smile.

My tongue swirls around him a few more times before I take him fully in my mouth. When I do, a loud hiss escapes his mouth. My head bobs as I suck his cock before I pull back slowly, teasing him. I repeat the process until suddenly, I am pulled up by my hair.

Leon, now inches from my face, whispers, "I'm going to fuck you now. Turn around."

Adrenaline runs through me as I do what I'm told. Even though we are in the shower and our bodies are wet, I can feel how soaked I am. Between sucking Leon's cock and him pulling me up by the hair to whisper demands, I am hot and horny.

Bent at the waist, Leon takes my hands, placing them against the tile. "Brace yourself."

The man doesn't give me much time to process his words because the second he lines his cock up at my entrance, he drives straight into me. A scream leaves my mouth. His movements are relentless. There is nothing gentle in the way he fucks me.

Just when I feel my hands start to slip down the steamy, wet tiles, Leon wraps a strong arm around my torso. He continues driving into me with a force I don't think I have ever known. That sweet pressure begins to build in the pit of my stomach.

"Rub your clit," he whispers into my ear. Even though his words are low, I hear the demand.

Loud and fucking clear.

I swear my heart rate spikes. His sultry words give me goosebumps. I will gladly follow this stranger's sexy demands.

Dragging my nails down the front of my body, I stop when I reach my clit. I touch myself, teasing before I begin to rub in a quick, circular motion. I can feel my pussy, tighten around him. I can't wait to reach that high that my mind and body currently crave.

"Good girl," is all he says while he grips me tighter, fucking me harder.

The second my orgasm starts to roll through my body, all coherent thoughts fade away. All I feel is good.

In the best way possible.

My hand falls away from my pussy as I continue to get lost in the pleasure. Leon has other plans, though, His fingers find my clit, continuing what I had started. My body shakes as another orgasm rips through me. I scream out his name while begging him to stop. That I can't take anymore.

"I can't, Leon, please."

"One more, baby."

He hikes my hips up, filling me fully with his cock. He pumps in and out fast. Hitting that sweet spot once again., This time, I swear I see stars. Hell, not only do I see the stars, I see the moon too.

I relish in the way my body comes alive. The way he makes me feel. It is truly indescribable. Even as I come back down to earth, I feel alive in only a way Leon can make me feel.

That should scare me.

I have been with many men, and not a single one has ever made me feel as good as Leon has this evening.

seven

. . .

I zip my bag close and go to hoist it up on my shoulder, but Leon stops me, taking it from my hands.

"Allow me."

He smiles, and it's genuine, as if we are not two strangers who agreed to a one-night stand.

After our shower, Leon talked me into staying with him for the evening. I, of course, agreed. I may be sore between my thighs, but I am not going to turn down more of whatever the man is about to dish out. With Callia occupied with her fake date, it was easy to say yes.

We make our way back out of my room. I wanted to grab a few toiletries because you never know. And since I'm on vacation, I might as well enjoy this little winter fling.

Once we step into the elevator, he leans in close, kissing on my neck. I turn into him to capture his lips with my mouth. Our kiss is slow, innocent at first, but quickly grows to something more. Something like hunger.

Suddenly, someone clears their throat.

Instantly, Leon and I step apart. We were so lost in each other that we did not notice the elevator come to a stop. Never even knew the doors opened.

There stands my best friend, Callia, with a shocked expression on her face.

"Excuse us— "

"Oh hey, Callia!"

Wow. This couldn't get any more awkward.

"We were just going." I try to keep a huge smile on my face.

I watch as her eyes flick between the two of us. She pauses on the bag that sits upon Leon's shoulders.

She knows my plans. A simple one-night stand.

"How was your date? The fake date?" I ask in a weak attempt to take some of the heat off me.

"It was good, fun."

Hmm... I tilt my head, assessing her. I think she had sex, though I can't be sure. We expect this behavior from me. Callia, not so much.

I have questions, and lots of them.

I'll have to get answers later, though, because time alone with Leon awaits.

"We were going to go to Leon's room for a little bit, but if you need me, I can stay back."

"No." Callia gives a fake laugh, and I wonder if it is fake because she was just out pretending with some dude.

"You two go on. I am tired, probably just gonna go to bed."

Something is up. I can feel it. I narrow my eyes. What am I missing?

Whatever she is keeping from me, we will be discussing in the morning. That I know for sure.

Leon clears his throat, distracting me.

"You are welcome to join us."

What?!

Callia looks mortified as she shakes her head before disappearing down the hall. She didn't even bother getting on the elevator. I laugh even though I'm a bit surprised by his words.

The elevator doors shut, and I turn to Leon.

"Are you into threesomes, orgies?"

He shrugs. "Maybe. If the right situation arises."

Hot damn! Hearing that from an older man shocks me.

Maybe I have met my match.

"Come on, Mariana! Let's go skiing."

Someone nudges me. That someone being my best friend.

Ugh.

I groan and attempt to roll away from her. I had a wild night with Leon. One that I hope to remember for a long time. I snuck back in just after six am. My entire body aches in the best possible way. I can feel the bruises on my hips, thighs.

Thoughts of Leon gripping my inner thighs to hold me still while he ate my pussy run replay in my mind.

More nudging.

"We only have a few more days here. No time to waste."

Callia is right. There is no time to waste.

Sighing, I slowly wake, stretching and rubbing my eyes.

"What time is it?" I ask.

"It's nearly noon. We can grab something quick from the cafe before heading out."

"Fine."

"Yay!" Callia is all excited, and I can only hope that I find some sort of caffeine soon because being exhausted on vacation is not an option.

I slowly drag myself out of bed and head for the bathroom.

After a very hot shower and some makeup, I am finally starting to feel more awake. Dark eyeliner and mascara make my green eyes pop.

I emerge from the bathroom to see Callia sitting on the edge of the bed. Callia is beautiful, plain, and simple. She does not have to apply makeup.

I study her for a minute more. She is hiding a secret.

One I intend to pry from her while we go skiing.

eight

· · ·

"So, what happened last night?" I ask.

"Nothing. We went to dinner, and that was it."

My hand darts out, hitting the button in the elevator. "Don't lie. You are not one to run off with a stranger. You looked flushed when I saw you. Something happened."

Callia sighs. "Fine, we went to dinner and had sex. I ran out after."

"You what?!" There is no way my best friend went and had sex with someone she doesn't know. No fucking way.

"Callia! You had a one-night stand? With a stranger? Did you use protection?" I blurt out the first thing that comes to my mind, though a hundred more questions are demanding to be asked.

"Yes, God, yes. Do you think I am dumb?" She sounds offended.

"Well, you did something reckless. Normal for me, maybe, but you? No. This is so not like you. Was he at least hot?"

"Oh, he was hot. So damn hot."

"What did he look like?" I continue prying. This is huge!

The elevator comes to a halt, and I worry our conversation will have to wait. Ugh.

The doors open, and a hot-ass man with blonde hair and the bluest eyes I've ever seen stands before us. I can't help but notice his reaction. Callia stiffens next to me.

I turn to look at her. What is this?! Her cheeks grow red.

Just as the doors go to close, he throws his hands out and steps in.

"Callia." The man nods and turns away from us.

She stands there, mouth agape.

No fucking way!

There's no way that Callia's one-night stand just stepped into the same elevator as us. I stare at my best friend. I wait for her to look my way, to say something. She doesn't.

"Is that him? The guy you screwed last night?" I whisper, even though I know it is pointless. There is no way he didn't hear me.

Callia elbows me.

"Oh, my lord! It is him. Isn't it?" I blurt. It must be. There is no way she would elbow me if not.

She just shakes her head, still refusing to look at me.

I'm about to ask another question, but the doors start to open. The gorgeous man darts his hand out, hitting a button. He turns to us.

"Yes, I'm the guy Callia fucked last night." He pauses. "She let me fuck her, and then she took off."

Holy shit!

Callia cringes while I stand there in complete shock at this man's words.

My best friend did what?! This is huge news! I need all the deets! Details I don't think Callia wants to discuss.

He seems upset over her taking off. But why?

"Callia! Was he bad in bed? This is so not like you."

That catches her attention. She jerks her head to look at me.

"What? No. That's not what . . . can we just not talk about this?"

Her dark eyes beg me to drop this conversation, and I will for now. For her sake, I will save all the questions for when it is just the two of us.

When we come to a stop at the lobby, the man turns to look at Callia. Bright blue eyes penetrate her soul before looking at me.

"If you figure out why she ran off, let me know."

I nod, unable to form a single word. Damn, he is blunt. But what's more, he clearly wants to know why Callia left after they did the deed. It is as if he actually cares.

Callia looks ashamed or maybe embarrassed.

I'm not sure, neither is something she expresses often. Callia does not stray or do reckless things.

She saves that shit for me.

Wrapping my arm through hers, I smile. "You can tell me all about it on the ski lift."

nine

. . .

"Wanna grab a hot chocolate?"

"Duh!" I laugh. Callia knows me too well. The sun was already starting to set as we made our way back to the Gravity Ski Lodge. A chill has set in my bones. I will gladly take a hot drink right now.

Skiing was a complete disaster, yet so much fun at the same time. I also got the full story from her about the delicious man we saw in the elevator. All I'm going to say is Callia is a mess.

We both grab our hot chocolates and head to the front of the cafe where the registers are. I spot her fake date before she does. I elbow her discreetly to get her attention. Callia looks up, noticing him. He's hard to miss.

"What?" she asks as she narrows her eyes at me.

"You should at least explain to him. Tell him about Juan and how you have never had a one-night stand."

She sighs and says nothing.

Just when I think she is going to drop it and just move on, she speaks up.

"Fine, meet you back in the room?"

"Uh, actually, would you be okay if I caught up with Leon for a little while?"

He snapped me, asking when he could see me again, and since we are both on borrowed time, I thought, why not? I might as well have a little fun while on winter break.

"Yeah, go. I could use some time to clear my head." She sounds sad.

I don't tell her that Dane has walked up behind her. His eyes are trained on her and only her.

"Clear your head from what?" he asks.

I go silent as I watch the scene begin to play out in front of me. Better yet, now is my time to leave. I smile and give a wave before leaving as quickly as possible. Callia has a mess to sort. I, on the other hand, have a mess to get into.

As soon as I reach Leon's door, I knock three times. Excitement runs through me. I will admit I have no desire for a relationship or anything more. I know this is nothing short of a fling. I am perfectly okay with that.

When Leon opens the door, I take him in. He is wearing casual clothes now. Jeans and a hoodie, yet he looks so hot.

"I've been waiting for you."

"Have you?" I tease as I pass over the threshold into his room.

"Yes."

"Good thing I'm here now."

The man wastes no time, wrapping an arm around me to pull me close to him. When he does, his delicious, manly scent invades my thoughts. While different from yesterday, it is natural, yet fresh. Still, I like it.

"How long do I have you this time?" he asks as he pulls away, his accent rolling off his tongue.

"That depends. What do you have in mind for this evening?"

"You, of course."

I remove my coat and smile at his blunt statement. I like how he doesn't beat around the bush. He is very straightforward, much like myself.

The man knows what he wants.

Maybe that's been my issue with me. None of the other guys I have hooked up with seem to know what they want. *They must still be boys*, I tell myself.

"Take off your clothes. I want to see you naked."

Leon is all man. There is no denying it. He doesn't ask, he demands. I think that's what I am enjoying most about this fling. For once, it is not me calling the shots.

Once I am naked, Leon pushes my dark hair off my shoulder. He places a soft kiss on the spot where my hair just was. His hand snakes down my chest, his fingers twisting and pulling at my taut nipples. His other hand reaches between my thighs, and a finger dips inside of me. I grind into him, wanting more.

The anticipation of what's to come thrills me.

"Already so wet for me," he says while adding a second digit.

I moan in response as I tilt my head back. He pumps his fingers a few times before pulling them out. When he does, I am left feeling empty.

"Leon?"

"Let's take this to the bed." He nods toward the bed. The same one he fucked me on last night. The only difference is this evening, the bed is made perfectly. Housekeeping must have come by. A giggle escapes me as I climb onto the bed while I think of how pointless that was of them.

"What is so amusing?" Leon asks with mischief in his eyes.

Making myself comfortable, I bend my knees and spread my legs, allowing him to get a good look.

"Oh, I was just thinking of how silly it was of housekeeping to make up your bed. We are bound to wreck it."

"I like how you think, Marina," he says as he starts to undress.

An idea suddenly comes to my mind, and I scoot closer to the edge of the bed. I grab a few pillows and prop them behind me.

Once I am comfortable, I slide my hand over my chest and pinch my nipple. Leon's eyes follow my hands as I move my hand down my stomach to my core. I dip a finger in, getting it nice and wet before I start rubbing my clit.

His cock jumps, his eyes are wild.

"Come, Leon, drop to your knees. I want you to watch as I touch myself."

Without hesitation, Leon drops to his knees. His face is now even with my pussy. He inhales deeply, drinking in my arousal.

Bringing my finger to his mouth, I force him to open. He sucks as I mimic what his cock will be doing to my pussy before too long.

Once I'm satisfied that it is good and wet, I pull it out and start rubbing my clit again.

"Marina," he growls. His eyes are trained solely on my pussy and what I am doing to myself.

I had no intention of taking the lead tonight. However, I am enjoying seeing this side of him. I need this control. I crave it. Based on how wet I am, I'd say my body wants it too.

I start to feel that indescribable pleasure begins to build. I am not sure if it is because I'm rubbing myself with the perfect amount of pressure or the fact that Leon is getting a close-up view of me masturbating. Either way, I am fucking ready to go.

Little moans leave my mouth as I throw my head back. I feel myself on the verge when, out of nowhere, Leon grabs my hand, stilling me. His mouth lands on me. He sucks and circles my clit with his skillful tongue until my hands fist his hair. I cry out as my orgasm explodes. I fuck his face while riding the waves. My thighs squeeze his cheeks tightly.

"Fuck me, Leon! Fuck me now!"

He pulls back, gripping my hips. He yanks me

even closer to the edge of the bed. I feel as though I may fall off, but Leon is quick. He stands tall, throwing my legs up over his shoulders. He positions himself at my entrance and pauses.

"Is this what you want?"

"Yes," I breathe out rapidly.

He takes a hand and spreads my lips. He thrusts in just enough that I can only feel the head of his cock. It is pure agony, this tease. It's something I never knew I craved until now. I lift my hips, and he pushes the rest of the way in.

And then he fucks me into the early winter morning.

ten

. . .

"Come to the slopes with me."

"I probably should get back to Callia." I feel bad enough that I have been so consumed with this man.

Leon rubs his chin as he studies me. "Didn't you say she had some things to sort with her fake date?"

"Well, yeah. But I think they are becoming more than just a fake date. I think the guy really likes her."

"In the same way I like you?"

I wave him off. "Not the same. We are just enjoying this little winter fling or whatever you want to call it."

His eyes narrow. I swear there is a tic in his jaw. He shakes it off fast.

"Come on, let's go out. Even if it is only for half a day, I'll have you back so you can do dinner with your friend."

"Deal."

As soon as we step onto the gondola that will take us up the slopes, Leon leans in close. He places a kiss on my cheek.

"You are so beautiful, Marina."

His compliment catches me off guard. If my cheeks weren't already rosy from the cold air, they sure are now. I'm not one who needs to hear such things. Especially if they are empty-handed comments, I do not need feelings, don't need attachments.

It's my preferred method. My mind and heart stay safe that way. So why am I unsure about how his words make me feel?

Now should be no different.

"Oh, Leon." I smile, turning into him. His lips land on mine, and off we go.

As we go higher, our kiss grows deeper. He gently grasps my chin, holding me to him. Even with his gloves on, this feels intimate.

"I mean it. You are the most beautiful woman I have had the pleasure of spending time with."

Fuck it, I decide to humor him. "Is that so?"

"Yes, I have no reason to lie. Right? This is just a fling to you, no?"

Well, shit, when he says it like that. I nod, not wanting to say the words out loud.

Leon's hand trails from my chin down the base of my throat, over my chunky plaid scarf.

"Tell me, Marina, have you ever done anything

risky in one of these in the middle of the day?" He looks around, referencing the gondola.

I swallow.

"Uh, no. I can't say that I have. Why?"

Leon does not respond, he only nods as he uses his teeth to remove one of his gloves. As soon as he has it off, he is back on me, kissing me. He pulls my scarf loose, kissing down the base of my throat. His hand snakes up under all my layers, and he wastes no time yanking my bra down to pebble my nipple between his fingers. His touch is ice cold at first, but it's quickly replaced with warmth. A warmth that starts to spread throughout my body.

The glass on the gondola has started to fog up. I wonder if people who pass by can see what we are doing. Maybe they assume.

"Lean back," Leon says as he pulls me forward and twists me to where I'm now sitting horizontally. He yanks his other glove off and tosses it to the floor. While I can't be certain of what his plans are, I have a pretty good guess.

Leon unbuttons my snow pants and dips his hand under my waistband. As soon as his fingers connect with my skin, I let out a quiet hiss. His fingers trail deeper until they reach my slit. Pushing a finger inside, he smiles a devilish grin at me.

"We only have minutes until we reach our destination." He pumps a finger in and out while his thumb rubs over my clit.

Minutes. He said minutes.

Panic tries to rise at the thought of being caught. I should be worried, but my body chases that familiar high.

"Leon," I half whisper as lust clouds my thoughts.

"Yes, love?"

Wait, did he just use the L-word?

"No—"I start to protest the use of that word, but his other hand dips back under my clothing. His fingers move so delicately over my breasts. All the while he continues to finger fuck me.

I'm close, so close. Yet the paranoid thoughts keep trying to seep through. Between getting caught and him saying that word, I can't quite let myself go.

"I'm close, but . . ." I breathe out heavily.

"Come all over my fingers," he says as he pinches my nipple tightly.

And I do.

The sparks fly as I contract around his finger.

I scream out his name as I come apart in our red gondola. Gone are the thoughts of being caught, wondering if anyone suspects a thing. Gone is that four-letter word.

I no longer care.

I open my eyes as Leon lets out a low chuckle. He pulls his fingers out from my pants and brings them to his mouth. He sucks the digit he used to get me off.

"You taste just as beautiful."

He winks before I hear a commotion. I look out the window and realize we have entered the docking station.

That was close.

Hot, but oh so close.

eleven

. . .

The snow has started falling softly. I keep wiping it away each time it hits my face.

My body is aching. Between Leon trying to teach me how to really ski, as opposed to my and Callia's way, and the bitter cold that has seeped into my bones, I am sore. What I wouldn't give to soak in a hot tub right now.

Too bad Callia and I didn't splurge on an upgraded room. My thoughts are cut short when I hear Leon clear his throat.

"Marina, my love." He pauses.

There is that word again. I stop in my tracks. Leon holds up his hands.

"Hear me out, please." He lets out a chuckle. He is nervous. "I feel this connection to you. You are different than anyone I have been with. These trips, I typically only spend one night with a woman. While I hate to admit that, it is the truth."

Where pleasure was earlier, dread starts to fill

me. Maybe I gave him the wrong impression. There is no way this will be anything other than a fling.

"I know it does not seem realistic, but I would like to continue seeing you. Even after I head back."

Now, it's my turn to chuckle.

"Leon, you can't possibly think we will be anything more than this." I point between us. "You live across the ocean. It would never work. Besides, I don't do relationships in general."

I start walking again. I can't stand to be outside for much longer. I want to be inside where it is warm.

I wish I could explain to him that my heart has been broken one too many times. The last relationship did me in. I was engaged until I found out my ex-fiancé only proposed because he witnessed the pressure from my family. I became unengaged after I learned that little fact.

Then, to try explaining the pressure to settle down and marry from my family. Yeah, no thanks. That would surely be a recipe for disaster. I happen to prefer getting laid over chasing the man off.

Would Leon even understand why I am this way? Probably not, so it is best I don't try to explain.

"I understand that. I just had to make it known how I felt."

Great, now I feel bad. I turn to face the gorgeous man.

"Look, let's spend our last night together. We'll

make it a night to remember, and then we will part ways."

Leon nods even though I know he wants to say more. I can see it written on his face. It is on the tip of his tongue. He says nothing. Instead, like the gentleman he is, he guides me the last few blocks to the resort with his hand resting just above my ass.

This I can do.

That other shit? Nope. Can't do it, won't do it.

Callia was not in our room when I popped in to gather up a few things for my last night with Leon. Part of me wants to cancel and just hide in the room until he leaves. That is not very realistic, considering I don't actually know when he leaves. And staying in this room for the next twenty-four hours is not an option.

So, I opt for one more night of fun in hopes that things will not be awkward between the two of us. Worst case, I can always bail and come back here.

I knock twice and wait. It is quiet on the other side. No sound of the television or anything. After I feel enough time has passed, I knock again.

Silence.

Maybe I misread him. I did say we would spend tonight together, right? I pull out my phone and open my Snapchat. There are no new messages from him.

I knock once more and decide to send him a

message through the app. I refused to give the man my actual number. It may seem silly, but I don't believe one-night stands or flings need to exchange phone numbers. I will gladly give out my Snapchat. I don't have my location on, so they can't even track me. Without a location or an area code, it makes finding me a tad difficult.

Just as I'm about to turn to leave, the door opens. There stands Leon in nothing but a towel. Water beads drip down his bare chest.

Fuck, why is he so hot?

Something like butterflies threaten to take flight, and I work hard to snuff them. Can't be having those exciting feelings with my little winter fling.

"Marina. I must apologize. I assumed you were coming later. I was just in the hot tub." He waves me in, holding the door out. "Please come join me. Do you have your suit?"

How did I miss him having a hot tub? I smile a wicked smile as I step into his hotel room.

"A suit won't be necessary."

As soon as he shuts the door, latching it, I know this will be a night to remember.

twelve

. . .

As I follow Leon through his suite, I look around. Clearly, I paid zero attention to the details of the room. We have always gone straight to his room and the ensuite bathroom. Now, though, I notice the decent-sized kitchenette. There's a small round table, two chairs. A small tan couch and an accent chair sit on the other side of the room. Paintings of what I can only assume are of Breckenridge hang on the walls. Leon comes to a set of sliding doors. I peer out, and that is when I see the hot tub. Steam rises from it. From here, I can see that there is a privacy panel that surrounds it from the suites on either side of him.

The snow is still falling. It is a surreal sight. Something this Florida girl is not used to seeing.

Leon walks up the two steps that lead into the hot tub. Just before he throws one leg over the side, he lets his towel drop.

He's naked.

And he's hard.

I stand there in awe of this man. This stranger. I may not know much about him at all, but one thing is for certain: he is comfortable in his own skin. I, too, am comfortable in my skin, I just don't flaunt it as casually. That could be because most men I hook up with could care less about what my body looks like. It's always just about sex and getting the dude off.

Leon is different from most men. So very different, and that part thrills me to no end.

Sadly, this will end. Leon, me, our little winter fling. It will soon become nothing but a distant memory.

"Join me, Marina." Leon is now fully in the hot tub. He holds out at hand.

I snap back into the present and quickly undress. I don't miss the low growl that leaves his lips, telling me he likes what he sees.

It is freezing out. Goosebumps prick my skin as I hurry up the steps to where the warm water waits.

I sink under until just my head is above the water. Instantly, I relax. The heat of the water is soothing to my cold bones.

"Feel better?"

I nod. "Yes, I am no longer freezing."

Leon chuckles at my admission and comes over close. His legs practically intertwine with mine. He leans in to kiss me, and I let him. I open willingly. Leon deepens the kiss while pulling me even closer to him. His erection grazes me, causing my body to react. It is as if my hips move on their own. He must take this as his cue because he pulls me with him until he is sitting on one of the seats. I straddle him. His cock is at my entrance. All I would need to do is shift a little.

Leon takes the lead. His hands slide along my back until they grab my ass, lifting me. He thrusts through my slit. I slide down to take him fully. Throwing my arms around his neck, I take a fistful of his dark hair. I want him to see me. I want him to remember how good our last time together is. I force myself to do the same.

It does not take long for us to find a steady rhythm. The bubbling water sloshes around, some of it falling over the side. Neither of us seems to care, though. We are both feeling good, relishing in the pleasure we both feel.

Leon arches slightly. The tingles in my spine climb to new heights.

Fuck, he feels amazing. This is the part I think I'll miss the most.

He leans in and takes my nipple between his teeth. At first, his tongue swirls around it, but then, after a moment, he applies pressure, biting down. I hiss out at first because of the instant pain, but it is soon forgotten as my orgasm nears.

My movements pick up. More waves crash over and out of the hot tub.

"Leon," I pant.

With my nipple still in his mouth, his other hand snakes up until his fingers find my other breast. He rubs my nipple between two fingers and pinches.

That's all it takes.

I scream out his name as I bounce harder than I think I ever have in my entire life. I am unable to control my motions. My orgasm has fully taken over every inch of my body.

I am vaguely aware that his lips and fingers are gone from my breasts. He grips me tightly. So tight, I think I may bruise. He continues thrusting as I am coming down from that blissful high. I am still pulsating around his cock when I hear a deep groan leave his lips. He pumps into me a few more times before slowing.

Leon lifts me so that he can slide out of me but holds me close. He peppers little kisses along my collarbone.

"Marina," Leon says with a serious tone.

"Hmm?"

"This can't be the last time we are together."

Sighing, I lean my forehead against his. Doesn't he get it? We live worlds away. Two very different lives.

"Leon," I start to protest, but he holds a finger to my lips.

"You feel it, do you not?"

Part of me has felt something. I squash it each time it bubbles up, though. I don't do relationships. I can't disappoint my family if I don't have a rela-tionship that will eventually fall apart. Love is a dangerous feeling. One I choose to avoid. Instead, I drift away, back to the opposite side of the hot tub. Back to where it is safe.

"Regardless of what I may or may not feel, you can't honestly think it will go far."

"It cannot go far if you do not allow it a chance. I am not a bad guy. You have enjoyed being with me."

"A little winter fling, remember?" I splash a little water his way in a poor attempt to lighten things up.

Leon moves fast. So fast, I don't have time to react. His strong arms wrap around my waist as he brings me close to him. I can feel every inch of his hard muscles that line his torso. The man is sexy as hell. There is no doubt about it. He can also fuck me in a way no other guy ever has. It must be his age.

"Fine. You may not want to give us a chance. I do. However, I will respect your wishes."

"Thank you," I murmur. Glad to be done with this heavy of a conversation.

That is until Leon clears his throat.

"Tonight, though, I will be having you as if you are mine."

He thrusts a finger between my folds. "Tonight, Marina, you are mine."

thirteen

. . .

I try hard not to digest Leon's words as he pulls me out of the hot tub. It is hard not to, though. While he wraps me in a fluffy white towel, all I hear is *tonight, Marina, you are mine.*

If he says anything more, I don't hear it. I'm too lost trying to wrap my head around his words. I am not *someone's.* When I did attempt past relationships, I never felt like I was *theirs.* Another reason it is better this way.

With Leon, though, *it feels different.*

I allow him to drag me through the suite and into the bathroom. I stand there in complete silence as he once again drops his towel. This time, however, I get a nice view of his ass. And what a nice ass it is.

He starts the shower, saying nothing. When he turns to look at me, my eyes meet his. I can't be sure, or maybe I want to deny what I see. Nevertheless, I see it.

There's determination and fire in those dark eyes of his. He holds my stare as if he is testing me. Hell, maybe he is.

Whatever it is, I try not to dwell on it. My heart rate, on the other hand, tells me differently. Feelings that threaten to take flight. Squashing them is the way to go.

It's all I know.

After a few more seconds of our intense stare-down, Leon clears his throat. He grabs my wrist, not gently, but not in a way that hurts me. I let him drag me into the shower even though the white towel is still wrapped around me. He stands me just under the spray of hot water.

In one swift move, he yanks the towel open and pulls it away from my body. I watch in unexpected shock as he tosses it aside.

"You no longer need that."

I swallow. He has a point.

A very valid point.

A point that awakens that sweet spot between my legs. I watch his black eyes assess my naked and very wet body. I swear they dilate before he rushes up on me. He comes up so fast that I nearly squeak. He pushes me back against the wall and grinds his evident erection against me. My body, in response, grinds back. I can give back whatever it is he plans to dish out.

His fingers find my pussy. Ever so slowly, he begins to tease me. Rubbing my clit in such slow motions that I have to fight the urge to beg him.

Leon leans in close, nipping at my ear. "Mine," he says as he hikes my leg up over his thigh. His fingers spread my lips wide before I feel his cock right there. He rubs his tip back and forth.

Dammit if he is not the best tease I have ever had.

"Leon," I moan out.

"Mine, Marina," he says as he gives me an inch. My eyes fall closed. Agony and pleasure mix. I fear I may succumb to his dirty tease just so I can feel as good as I know he can make me feel.

"Mine," he grits out once more.

His determination to stake claim on me has me feeling all sorts of ways. Ways I am unsure of. Ways I'm not entirely sure of what to do with them.

He gives me another inch, and I try hard to get more of him. He grips my hips too tightly, though. He holds me in place.

I both hate it and love it.

Without warning, Leon drives into me hard. I scream out. He pumps into me maybe three times before he pulls almost all the way out.

"Leon!" I all but beg.

He gives me a nudge.

Fuck! The man is teasing me badly. I attempt again to move against his body. However, he is stronger than me. He makes it look effortless with the way he keeps me in place.

He pulls all the way out of me. I whimper in protest.

"Leon."

"Tell me I am yours for tonight."

I lean my head back to take a good look at the man. It is then that I see it. There is a fire there that I did not notice before. Or maybe I was in denial. I can't be sure.

Right now, though, in this raw moment, I see Leon's thoughts loud and clear.

The man wants my body.

He not only wants my body, he also wants me.

I chew on my bottom lip. I can give him tonight. What is the worst that can happen?

"Fine, tonight I'll be yours. Tonight only."

A sinister smile appears across his lips. "We'll see about that."

I go to laugh but am cut off when his lips capture mine. He kisses me so fiercely that I think I may burn.

And I very well may.

fourteen

. . .

Leon thrusts the rest of the way into me. I can't help but moan out. His movements are different. Maybe it is the air between us. I don't know, I can't quite explain it. It's just different.

"Touch yourself for me," he demands.

I nod because, after all, I am his tonight. My hand falls from around his neck to my pussy. I reach between our bodies and find my clit. I start with little circles. I tease myself just enough to bring me to the brink, and then I stop.

Leon must notice. He halts his movements.

"Did I say stop?"

"No," I reply.

"Don't stop until I say to."

Instantly, my fingers begin to move again. Fuck. How does he make his demands sound so hot?

He is ruthless as he pounds into me. Thrust after thrust. My legs begin to shake as I try to keep up with his momentum. It's hard, though. He's rough and hard with me. His hands grip the underside of my thighs so tight, promising to leave more marks. I welcome them because that means tomorrow when this is all over, I'll remember him. I'll remember our time together.

"Mine," he growls into my ear.

His words serve as a warning, but my orgasm extinguishes it as I come apart. My hand falls from between us, and he grabs it fast.

"I didn't say stop touching yourself." He jabs my hand back at my pussy.

"Leon, please," I beg.

"Don't stop."

With his hands over mine, I start rubbing circles over my sensitive nub. Each time he thrusts, my finger rubs harder.

Within seconds, I am screaming out his name again. My entire body shakes. All the while, he keeps his hand over mine, guiding me. He doesn't let me go.

"Leon! Please! I can't take anymore!"

My entire body is on sensitivity overload. I cannot take anymore.

"You may stop."

I let out a shaky sigh of relief when his hand drops away from mine.

He pulls out of me suddenly. "On your knees."

I tilt my head, unsure if I heard him right. He starts shoving my shoulders down, confirming I did, in fact, hear him just fine.

Leon grabs a fistful of my dark hair and yanks back slightly. It causes my eyes to water, not that he can probably see because the spray of the shower continues to fall over us.

He lines his cock up with my mouth, forcing me to open for him. He is gentle at first. Slow thrusts. After what my body just went through, I will take whatever kind of slow he dishes out.

All too soon, though, his grip on my hair tightens, and he picks up the pace. Thrusting harder and harder as he fucks my face. My eyes continue watering as he forces me to match his movements.

The man gives no warning when he finally explodes in my mouth. Warm spurts of cum hit the back of my throat as I swallow. I milk every last salty drop.

"Mine," he grunts once last time before he pulls out of my mouth. I wipe whatever has dripped out with the back of my hand.

To any other woman, this might come across as degrading. Not to me, though. I love it

Dare I say that word?

He does not give me time to think about that word. He pulls me up swiftly. I meet his lustful gaze. The way he is rough with me is something I didn't know I would enjoy.

Boy, do I enjoy it.

He grips my chin and kisses me hard. Even though I just had his cock in my mouth along with his cum. He doesn't seem to give two shits. Most guys would never.

There is something about the way he kisses me. Something I don't want to admit, maybe.

Leon is the first to pull away. "I know I said we had tonight, but I must be going."

I nod in surprise. This ending stings a bit. I don't want him to know that, so I put on my best smile.

He kisses me again. As if he knows this will be our last kiss, and he is making sure to memorize it.

It will be after all.

When he finally pulls back, I remind myself to breathe and to calm down. He turns and shuts off the shower. I watch as he climbs out first. He comes back with a towel. He holds it out, and I take it. The guilt of not wanting to take this further threatens to eat me.

Damn him for doing his best at cracking my hard exterior.

Once we are both dressed, he walks me to the door.

"Marina, I hope you change your mind, but in case you do not, I want you to know that I have enjoyed my time with you. You are unlike any other."

I smile yet say nothing. There is nothing that I can say to make this ending hurt a little less.

Nothing at all.

He must sense that and nods his head. I step out into the quiet hallway. It's late. Leon places one last kiss on the corner of my lips before shutting the door, effectively ending us and our fling.

I walk back to my hotel room and replay the last

days over and over. By the time I reach my and Callia's room, I smile.

One thing is for sure: the man can fuck like no other, and I'm sure going to miss our little winter fling.

acknowledgments

ARC readers - Thank you for continuing to read my stories.

Readers - I can't tell you how thankful I am that you have chosen to read my words. Without you, there would be no me. Thank you.

To my romance babes - Ya'll are the best! Thank you for your support over these last four years!

To B.A. - I love that I can reach out to you anytime! Your tips and expertise play a vital role in certain scenes!

also by lisamarie kade

The Secrets We Keep

Mended Hearts

The War Within

The Surprise Within

The Christmas Breakdown

Shattered Illusion: The Red Society Book One

Shattered Reality: The Red Society Book Two

A Little Winter Romance

about the author

Lisamarie Kade is a romance author living in the Sunshine State with her husband and small army of children.

When not writing, she can be found chasing the kids around or volunteering for one of their many activities.

Lisamarie enjoys chocolate peanut butter cups, music, and reading something steamy while sipping an alcoholic beverage.